A Day of Ochre, Ascending

A Day of Ochre, Ascending

Rick Powell
WRITER

Marie Moldovan   Joe Mykut

EDITORS

Joseph Mykut -Editor, cover inspiration and concept contribution.

Marie Moldovan - Editor, Publication Layout, Illustrations, and cover design.

A Day of Ochre, Ascending

I Ain't Your Marionette Press, P.O BOX 184, Larder Lake ONTARIO, P0K 1L0, Canada.

ISBN: 978-1-998213-26-9

To the world,
A realm of shadows and whispers,
where beauty and terror intertwine.
For the dark mysteries that haunt our
nights and the fleeting moments of
light that guide us through the abyss.
May we find the strength to navigate
through the chaos of connection.

FOREWORD

It is with pleasure that I introduce "A Day of Ochre, Ascending," an apocalyptic tale inspired by Robert W. Chambers' "The King in Yellow." This gripping narrative, penned by the Father of Mannequins, Rick Powell, takes readers on a journey through a world about to be baptized by hell.

The story begins with Walter taking a leisurely stroll with his dog, Archie, and quickly descends into a nightmare. As the day unfolds, Walter finds himself ensnared in a series of terrifying events that challenge his reality.

Drawing inspiration from Chambers' haunting work, this tale delves deep into the human psyche, exploring themes of fear, madness, and the unknown.

Powell's prose welds readers to their seats, unable to escape the unfolding horror.

"A Day of Ochre, Ascending" is a profound exploration of the human condition in the face of terror. Powell's ability to evoke a sense of dread and unease is unparalleled, making this a must-read for fans of supernatural horror.

I have had the privilege of offering editorial advice for this remarkable book to the publisher, and I am honored to present "A Day of Ochre, Ascending" to you. I have no doubt it will leave a lasting impression on all who dare to read.

~Pita Black of Cranberree Ink

INTRODUCTION

In the eerie and unsettling world of "A Day of Ochre, Ascending," Rick Powell weaves a tale that draws inspiration from the haunting works of Robert W. Chambers. This short horror story plunges readers into an apocalyptic nightmare, where the ordinary quickly transforms into the extraordinary.

Walter, our protagonist, begins his day with a simple stroll with his dog, unaware that he is about to descend into a realm of terror that defies comprehension. As the ochre skies loom overhead, the boundaries between reality and nightmare blur, leading Walter—and the reader—into a chilling journey that questions the very fabric of existence.

Rick Powell's writing style is characterized by its dystopian undertones and atmospheric depth. He excels at creating worlds that are both familiar and disturbingly alien, drawing readers into settings where societal collapse and existential dread are palpable. His prose is both evocative and precise, painting vivid images of desolation and despair while maintaining a gripping narrative pace.

Powell's ability to blend the mundane with the macabre makes his stories uniquely compelling. His characters often find themselves in situations that challenge their perceptions of reality, forcing them to confront their deepest fears. In "A Day of Ochre, Ascending," Powell's dystopian vision is brought to life through his meticulous attention to detail and his talent for building suspense, ensuring that readers are both captivated and unnerved from beginning to end.

Prepare to be captivated and unnerved as you step into a world where the familiar becomes the fantastical, and the mundane is anything but.

~*Marie Moldovan*

"We sink into the depths of blood when we speak before we think."

~ Marie Moldovan, 2024

There was a stillness to the day that was hard to define as he took his dog for a walk that morning. The tranquility seemed to hang in the air, a rare moment of peace amidst his usually busy life. He finally had an extra day off from his maintenance job at the plant, and the early summer day was his to enjoy—within the limits set by his wife, of course.

He knew he should get more exercise, and their Welsh terrier, Archie, was also starting to show signs of weight gain. Harriet often remarked that the dog was a reflection of its owner, suggesting that he use days like this to improve his fitness. After all, he wasn't getting any younger, and lounging around the house would only put him in the path of Harriet's cleaning spree.

After a small breakfast of eggs and toast, Walt put Archie on his thin leash and left the comfort of their

American colonial house. They started on the trek into the bright New England day, embarking on their familiar route.

As he passed by the many houses along the suburban street, Walt couldn't help but smile. Archie's little black tail was wagging, mirroring his owner's cheerful mood. The little dog trotted by Walt's side, eager for the smells and sights the walk would bring.

They encountered a cherub-faced woman with graying hair in curlers, shuffling out of her doorway to collect the morning paper. She offered a friendly grin and waved, holding her robe closed over her large form. Walt waved back, his spirits lifted by the simple exchange, and continued on his way.

Archie occasionally looked back at him, tongue hanging out and panting happily, as they treaded through the familiar streets. Feeling more adventurous than usual, Walt followed the sidewalk as it turned to the right and led them to the main street lined with a multitude of shops. A few he had visited with his wife on occasions when it warranted it, for the odd gift for a relative they barely talked to or forgetful items they needed.

As he passed the generic clothing shops and nail salons, he approached the junction of an alley. For no apparent reason, it seemed a small breeze was blowing out of the entranceway. A tattered page of the local paper came tumbling out, followed by some indescribable debris.

Archie, who usually chased any object smaller than himself, seemed to pause and sniff the air. A low growl emanated from his tiny throat, and they both froze in place.

Grasping the leash tightly, he sensed something huge, possibly a truck or other vehicle, waiting in the alleyway a dozen or so yards ahead of them.

It did not seem plausible since the narrow back street was barely wide enough for two individuals walking side by side to get through.

This slight hesitancy made him look around the area of the street, wondering if any other pedestrians seemed aware or if, by chance, they could see something coming out of the aperture. There was no one around to be seen. The cars that passed in the street adjacent to the alley made no indication that something or someone was exiting.

In the eerie silence, Archie's growl cut through the stillness, a harbinger of unseen dangers lurking in the shadows. Walt, poised to retreat, halted as a child's laughter, chillingly out of place, whispered through the air. The sound prompted Walt's gaze to dart toward the alley's entrance, despite the laughter seeming mere feet away. With cautious steps, he advanced toward the entrance, intermittently tugging at the leash to coax Archie forward. With each gentle pull, Archie issued a low growl yet moved with a stiff gait, matching Walt's tentative pace.

"Hello," Walt said, feeling awkward. He expected a child to come running out, which caused him a tinge of concern since this alley was so close to the main street. If someone were to rush out, the passing cars would likely not be able to brake in time.

He heard the laughter again, this time a little louder, as if all around him. The hairs on his neck stood up in some sort of display of nameless fear. He turned to the main street to see if there was any danger from passing cars if the unknown child came rushing out, but there was not a car in sight. This struck him as odd since the morning rush should be continuing in full force as it had been moments earlier.

He heard Archie bark and turned his head back in the direction of the alleyway.

The little girl was now standing there, motionless. She didn't look like any child he had ever seen before. The aged dress she wore looked like something from days long gone. The fabric seemed almost gossamer with age. The lace along the bottom and on the sleeves looked almost sun-bleached, as if it had been sitting for years.

The wrinkled lace on her shoulders and going up her small neck cast odd shadows on her skin in the morning light. It seemed as if a large cloud had passed overhead, giving her pale face and wide eyes a ghostly hue.

He questioned if the laughter had come from this little girl. Her expression was so forlorn and morose that he wondered if maybe another child had been tormenting her and had run off. It seemed unlikely since there was no other way out of the alleyway.

He took notice of the high, aged brick walls that surrounded the area and the chipped stone wall yards behind her.

"Are you lost, child?" he asked. A mysterious breeze from the alleyway caressed his brow, its origin unknown. It bore the musty scent of mold and the faint, unsettling odor of decaying meat. He wiped away a sudden cold dampness from his forehead, a sensation that had not been there moments before. "Do you have a home?"

She stepped out of the alleyway and moved toward him; her head cocked to the side oddly. It seemed almost like she was looking at a curious, unfamiliar object. Her blond, unwashed hair was tied in pigtails with blue ribbons as faded as her dress. "Lost?" she said. Her eyes, which were already dark, were made all the more dark by the shadow of the cloud that had seemed to encompass the morning so quickly. "We are all lost."

A low whine emanated from the throat of the terrier, but Walt was still mesmerized by the eyes and expression of the little girl. He looked down at her when she stopped a few feet in front of him. He noticed now that the shadow on her neck and clavicle was not from brittle lace but from some scar or brand that encircled her tiny throat underneath it.

It looked like an impression of a long leaf frond.

Walt looked both ways along the storefronts, abandoned by pedestrians of any sort. A chill covered his whole body as he looked down at Archie. The dog was lying flat on the ground, his small eyes looking up at Walt full of pity, and his ears were down, as if Walt had just chastised him. His sorrowful eyes left Walt's face and looked at the little girl, and he let out a sickly whine.

The little girl made no notice of the canine. She continued to scrutinize Walt's face. "You are lost now," she whispered.

He realized that she was holding an aged, hard-bound book in her lithe hand, which hung limply at her side. It was a gangrenous green with an illustration of a scorpion on the cover. The pungent odor of the breeze wafted again, and the book fell to the cracked pavement and opened up, the amber-colored pages flapping in the current of air. The girl did not even attempt to pick it up.

Walt crouched down to retrieve it as the girl's dark eyes never left his face. He glanced at the archaic pages and read a few of the sentences that were written there.

Camilla: *The suns have been swallowed by the darkness.*

Cassilda: *The Hyades are singing. Come, let us go! It shall not be missed.*

Camilla: *(frowning) It is unfair. Leaving this grand affair for another.*

Stranger: *I have many other affairs to show you. Look!*

Cassilda: *The lake! The lake is crimson!*

The book felt cold and clammy in his hands. He closed it and returned it to the girl. She raised it to her face, turning it over a few times as if she had just discovered it. Then, she looked at him and gave an evil smirk. He noticed that she hadn't blinked once during this entire time. Without a sound, she turned and disappeared back into the alley. The hint of sky overhead was now covered with a myriad of clouds that hadn't been there moments before.

"Wait, where are you going? What is your name?" he shouted. His voice seemed to echo back at him.

"Celia," she said, not turning as the hem of her dress fluttered in the breeze.

Archie started barking ferociously and struggled against his leash, pulling back as if to get free.

Walt bent down to grab Archie's collar and control the little dog before he could escape into the street behind them.

As he lifted the dog into his arms, he turned and looked into the alley.

He noticed that the breeze and stench were gone, just like the little girl.

***

He turned back towards home, relieved to be in the semi-clean air and light breeze when the first cramps hit his stomach. Holding Archie's still-barking leash with one hand, he placed his other hand on a grimy lamppost to steady himself until the nauseating feeling passed. The corkscrew-like pain had him almost doubled over in agony.

Harriet had better not have used expired eggs, he thought as he tried to catch his breath. His eyes were squeezed shut, and he was on the edge of panic when the feeling began to slowly pass. He opened his watering eyes and saw Archie's pitiful look. The dog let out a low whimper. His little tail was wagging, and he barked once, as if confused by his master's pale face.

Walt, panting, said weakly, "I am fine, you little beast. It'll pass. I just have to talk to your mistress when we get home." The little dog cocked his head, his tail wagging more. Walt turned his attention away from his furry companion and looked down at the ground, hesitant to straighten up. He feared that doing so would start the sharp pain again.

It was then that he noticed a sheet of yellowish paper flapping and stuck to the cuff of his pant leg. The parchment was wrapped around in such a way that it gave the illusion of some sort of leech or grub.

He felt a slight tightness around his shin. He looked at it questioningly as he reached down and peeled it off, feeling the cold dampness against his skin.

He straightened up carefully and inspected the paper. There was no discernible writing on the front, and the outer edges had a slight brownish hue, as if from the dust of years gone by. It had almost the texture of rice paper. As the slight wind flipped it over, it exposed two small tears that were almost like punctures from a child's fingers.

He gasped when the fluttering paper flew out of his hand, leaving behind a small cut on his palm, right below his thumb.

A small bead of blood appeared in the tiny gash, and he instinctively sucked away the sting in his hand.

Looking in the direction the page had flown, he saw it tumbling and wafting through the air, up into the clouds that were darker than before...

Spitting out pinkish saliva onto the sidewalk, Walt inspected the cut. A numb sensation lingered on his tongue. The bleeding had been brief, though the sting persisted.

Looking up at the heavy clouds, he murmured, "We better get home, my friend. The day is growing stranger."

In reply, the terrier barked as they left the lamppost and headed home. The pain from the cut overshadowed the dull cramp in his stomach, yet subconsciously, his hand remained pressed to his abdomen.

A sense of displacement troubled Walt, its cause elusive.

Glancing at the street, he pondered its unfamiliarity. The terrier's slower trot made him hesitate, almost tugging at the leash as the little dog moved with a frightened gait, its head swinging as if echoing Walt's unease.

Passing a nail salon, Walt noticed that the painted letters advertising prices and specials appeared faded, as though sun-bleached by years of exposure—an odd sight, given he recalled the store's recent opening.

Peering through the storefront's large glass pane, he saw no lights within, and the furniture seemed aged.

Movement flickered in the store's shadows, but he dismissed it as a trick of the clouds' reflection.

He hurried on, trying not to look at the other shops and ignoring the absence of cars on the streets as he pulled the tiny dog along; its tail and ears down as it tried to keep close to its master.

***

Nearing home, the cramps hit him again. They were not as painful as before but caused a tightness in his bowels that intensified the need for him to rush to the oval-paneled doorway as quickly as he could with Archie lagging. He considered picking the small dog up to carry him to the door but was worried that bending would cause more discomfort.

He tried to turn the door's knob, but it refused to turn in his clammy palm. Frowning, he realized he'd left his keys inside because there was never an occasion to lock it. The quiet neighborhoods in his part of town rarely faced break-ins or the violence common in busier parts. He knocked on the door and after a few moments, knocked louder.

"Harriet!" he shouted. "Harriet! I don't have my keys. Open the door!" His voice portrayed more fright than frustration.

Looking around at the other houses in embarrassment, he noticed not a soul was out or peering through curtained windows. The absence of neighbors matched the absence of sunlight as the day gradually turned grayer.

He glanced down at Archie, and the little dog looked up at him, its head cocked as if wondering why they hadn't entered yet.

Sensing movement, he looked up. Through the distorted, etched glass of the door, he saw his wife standing motionless. Her arms hung limp at her sides in the well-worn nightgown she always wore. Her head was pressed against the glass, making it seem as though she was peering at him through a microscope, and he was some alien amoeba.

More shocking than Harriet's stillness was the cadaverous look on her face—a look of apathy teetering on the edge of hopelessness. Her hair hung limply, and her eyes held a lifelessness he couldn't define. A chill swept over him, rendering him speechless. As he was about to call out to her, she stepped back, almost floating ethereally, into the dark recesses of their home.

"Harriet! H-H-Harriet?" His voice, laced with shock and fear, echoed as he hammered on the door, the urgency evident in the force of his fist. Meanwhile, Archie, caught up in the commotion, barked furiously at the end of his leash.

Suddenly, a high, piercing shriek came from within the house—a single wail of such agony that Walt staggered back in surprise. He heard a slight yelp from the little dog as he unknowingly dropped the leash. A chill enveloped his body from the horrendous sound that continued to emanate from inside.

Jesus Christ! he thought. *What the hell is going on here?*

He absently clutched his stomach, the cramping forgotten in the last few moments. He screamed her name a few more times, too afraid to even touch the door, regarding it as if it were some sort of diseased structure. Realizing the leash was no longer in his hand, he looked down at his feet, quickly scanned the area, and then turned to see Archie running down the sidewalk, the leash dragging behind him.

He yelled the dog's name and ran after him. Walt's frustration built, and the pain increased as he tried to call the dog back. This cannot be happening, he thought in panic. Each step sounded magnified, his thoughts swirling. He knew he should be breaking into his house to check on his wife instead of chasing after the dog. Had she suffered a stroke? A breakdown?

His concern was overshadowed by the fright he had felt at seeing her in those nightmarish moments. The look on her face was more malignant than pleading for help, almost as if she were someone else. Her one eye peering at him gave a flash of recognition, lost in the flurry of thoughts as he ran on.

As he turned the corner past the shops they'd passed before, he tried to rationalize. His wife was safe in the house. Archie had never been out free in all his years, especially not so close to the busy streets and intersections of their neighborhood. He wished now that he had gotten one of those cellular phones everyone seemed to have. Harriet had mentioned it numerous times. His thoughts froze, and he stopped, lungs burning as he tried to catch his breath, gazing down the shop-lined street.

The businesses and storefronts looked as though they hadn't been inhabited for years. Streetlamps at the intersections were dead black, without power, echoing the broken and neglected windows that lined the streets in either direction.

Some storefronts bore evidence of charring, and one coffee shop awning had lichen or mold trailing down from it, as if it had been growing for years.

In places, the pavement was marred by a black, oil-like substance that had burst forth, leaving behind a foul-smelling trail that had long since dried, leading towards already clogged street drains.

Debris and garbage were strewn everywhere, as if the Earth had regurgitated the city's trash back to its inhabitants.

Not a car or person was in sight. The only movement came from the occasional rocking of dead streetlights, as if nudged by some unfeeling breeze.

What the hell is going on? Jesus Christ! What is this? Walt's mind screamed. His heart pounded in his chest, adrenaline surging through his veins. How could this have happened in the few moments since he'd last passed down the street? *Dear God, I must be asleep, having a nightmare. Please, let this not be real.*

He heard a yelp and saw Archie being pulled into the same alleyway as before. The little dog struggled against the black, shining tendrils that dragged him into the dark recesses of the alley. Archie's fur smoked and seemed to burn as snake-like appendages wrapped tightly around him, pulling him away. Walt screamed and ran, his heart racing, oblivious to the wetness and odor that filled his trousers and ran down his leg as his bowels gave way.

Reaching the mouth of the alley, all he saw was a cavern of blackness, an entrance darker than any shop or storefront window. He heard Archie's whines, but the sound grew fainter, as if smothered by a sea of nothingness. Walt stood incredulous as the whining quickly fell silent.

Sweating and wide-eyed, he surveyed both sides of the apocalyptic roadway.

Then he rushed into the middle of the cold street and gazed at the clouded, gray sky overhead. Not a speck of star or moon was visible through the heavy, foreboding clouds that stretched for miles.

Tears rolled down his face as he took a deep breath and prepared to shout.

"HELP ME! SOMEONE! ANYONE! WHAT IN GOD'S NAME IS HAPPENING?!?"

His scream pierced the night air as he collapsed onto the cracked pavement, sobbing with his face in his hands.

"God?" A little girl's voice spoke.

Walt gasped and looked up, holding his breath as he stared a few yards ahead at the mouth of the black alley. Celia stood there, just as before, clutching the same book to her chest. She had the demeanor of a mischievous student who had arrived late to class without a care for the consequences.

"W-w-what has happened? What has happened to the world?" he sputtered, trying to control the sobs hitching in his chest.

"It is time. The King will be arriving. The tides of the Lake of Hali will be crashing in," she said, her voice echoing down the empty street.

Walt looked around in confusion. He felt as if his mind was slowly being ripped apart. He had a vague sensation that her words were recalling something deep in his soul, something at the edge of recollection, but he could not grasp it. He looked at her, his face a picture of hopeless despair.

With a sigh, she walked over to him as a cold wind began to blow all around the town. He heard cans and other assorted trash tumble around, as if insects scurrying in the dark. Celia stopped in front of him, looking down as if in contempt. She took the book she held so closely in her arms, opened it to the first page, and showed it to him.

"Read... and understand."

She turned the pages as he began to read. Initially, only a few words were discernible, blurred through his tear-filled eyes. Her hands moved gracefully, reminiscent of a mother teaching a child their first words. As his face dried, his reading grew more frantic. He lost track of time, unable to determine if he had been reading for minutes, hours, or days. It was unclear when he took the book from her hands and started turning the pages himself.

The book conjured visions of Hastur and the entities beneath the Lake of Hali. The sound of the twin suns sinking resonated with him. He absorbed every intricate detail of Carcosa and the nascent transformation of his world into a realm where the King would reign supreme. The whispered secrets of Camilla and Cassilda reached his ears, as if they were meant for him and him alone. The earth trembled beneath his knees, heralding the black void of the final act.

When he finally closed the book, he recognized the trembling as his own, not from the cold pavement where he knelt. However, the source of the noxious odor—whether from himself or the wind that began to buffet around him—remained uncertain.

His frail hands let the book drop as he turned his eyes toward Celia. She was now accompanied by what was once his wife and a large nightmarish beast. The bear-sized monstrosity might have once been covered in fur but was now covered in green-filled pustules and rope-like scars. The skin underneath looked charred. The scars on the monster resembled the tattoo-like 'fronds' on Celia. The red, bleeding eyes of the beast showed only a passing resemblance to the terrier that Archie once was.

"Why is this happening?! Why me?!" he cried out to her.

"Why not you? There is no reason. You are just a random choice. This world, this universe, was all created by random choices. This was all a random accident, really," her voice echoed.

The beast let out a howl that could only have been issued by something not of this world. With what the world was becoming, he was sure there would be other creatures making even more sounds beyond imagination soon enough. Its massive, misshaped paws scratched divots into the littered pavement as it shambled up next to Walt and lay down in supplication next to its master.

Walt's pale face turned down the darkened road. He could faintly discern a few forms silhouetted in the distance: dark shapes in an even darker blackness. What used to be the residents of his town had turned into beings too nightmarish to describe. The only recognizable one was the obese woman he had waved to that morning, but she had only had two arms then, and she hadn't been leaving a bubbling acid-like substance behind her when she walked.

As the whipping wind grew colder, he was knocked back by a piece of paper or cloth that hit him in the face. He squeezed his eyes closed from the pain as it adhered to his cheeks, like some sort of large insect or leech. He shrieked and fell to the ground.

His hands scrambled to tear the fabric away, but doing so only made him cry out louder. It felt like he was trying to tear his flesh off. He rolled on the ground, his fingers scrambling on the edges and hanging flaps of putrid-smelling material.

After a few moments, he moved his shaking hands away. He opened his watering eyes and realized he could see through crudely fashioned eye holes in the paper.

It was the paper from the book that had fluttered away before. The page from that cursed play was, in fact, now his mask.

His trembling grew more erratic as what was left of his sanity left him, and he started to chuckle.

He sat up and smiled at the misshapen forms as they slowly gathered around him in this cold, dark apocalyptic world.

He grasped at his soiled, tattered clothes, and his chuckles turned into unceasing laughter. His tearing eyes looked around in a frantic manner behind the eye holes of the mask; the mask that he now felt squirming on his face and would feel for all time.

He heard something clatter and roll in the increasing torrent of wind and felt it knock into his foul-smelling thigh. It was a large glass jar. Its stained, cracked glass showed evidence that it came from the scattered trash that filled the town. The trash that was now the world.

He picked it up and inspected it. The bottom was broken off and leaving nothing but jagged sharp teeth.

His last rational thought, before he raised the jagged teeth high to be one with the tender flesh of his pale head, was that every king needs a crown.

ACKNOWLEDGEMENTS

In the cringy corridors of creation, I owe my deepest gratitude to those who stood by me amidst the chaos.

To my family, your unwavering support has been the beacon in the shadows guiding me through the abyss.

To my editors, your sharp eye and relentless pursuit of perfection have breathed life into this tale of despair, unearthing the horrors that lurk within.

To my friends and beta readers, your honest critiques and steadfast encouragement have been the pillars of this journey, standing firm against the encroaching darkness.

And to you, the reader, for daring to traverse this dystopian landscape with me. Your courage and curiosity are the lifeblood of this story, illuminating the shadows and confronting the terrors that lie in wait.

~Rick Powell

ABOUT THE AUTHOR

Rick Powell

Rick Powell is a resident of Oak Forest, Illinois, U.S.A. Rick began writing horror and dark fiction in 2012. His poetic and narrative talents have graced the pages of various publications, including Infernal Ink Magazine and the tantalizing anthology Lustcraftian Horrors: Erotic Stories Inspired by H.P. Lovecraft.

ABOUT THE EDITORS

Joseph Mykut

Joseph Mykut is a native of Alabama. They are an author, artist, illustrator, editor, photographer, and agent. Their artwork and photography are on display internationally in Ontario, Canada and can be found in the anthologies **3 Amigos Ink and Splatter Lonely Soul in the**

Darkness, *The Way of the Crow and Shattered Psyche*. All anthologies are **I Ain't Your Marionette Press** publications out of Canada. They also authored and illustrated the children's book, "Beautiful Boy", of the same publishing house.

Joseph's art and photography uniquely focuses on the random, seemingly unimportant aspects of the everyday environment surrounding us. They hope this draws attention to the deeper details that express the magic and beauty in the otherwise mundane.

As a member of the LGBTQ2+ community as well as walking the path of Shamanism, they hope to create and represent a more tangible bridge between the physical life experience and the world beyond our physical senses.

Joseph was born and raised in the deep south of the United Sates in what's known as the bible belt. His influences have developed over time to be more of the universe and of spirituality rather than religion.

However, Joseph is an ordained minister with the Universal Life Church as it aligns with his perspective that there is truth found in all religious beliefs as they are all smaller pieces to a greater picture.

They identify as a two spirited being or even multi spirited being and identify with all ideas of the gender spectrum. They believe in the existence of both light and dark or positive and negative energies leaving the truth of who we are to be found in the balance of those energies

Marie Moldovan

Marie Moldovan is a Saskatchewan native and Ontario immigrant. Some would call them a reverse snowbird, who feels most comfortable surrounded by snowcapped mountains.

Nomadic by nature, Marie is multifaceted and has mastered many skills. They dub themselves a jack of many trades and master of some. However, because Marie has acquired a plethora of diplomas spanning the educational spectrum, Marie's mother on the contrary would call them a professional student.

Marie would accredit their adaptability to the training they received as a Canadian Forces medic, and their artistic ability to their family. Both attributes have aided her along their journey from the points of homelessness and despair to the place of stability and optimism Marie has arrived at today.

In 2018, Marie was diagnosed with service-related PTSD, and within the same breath of time became a widow.

Unresolved trauma, and the loss of their husband caused Marie to skirt the edges of insanity. Faced with losing complete touch with reality, they returned to writing and art.

In a sense writing and art saved Marie's life, at least that's their claim. Fortunately, for the world, Marie's choice to embrace creation has led them to captain a new life as a publisher, illustrator, writer and artist.

Marie is the author of **20 years of Winter, Miss Sally Anne** and has currently opened the doors of her own publication organization, aptly named, **I Ain't Your Marionette Press**.

20 Years of Winter is an autobiographical collection of poetry and art. She published it in hopes to make a way for others who have suffered similar traumas to feel safe knowing that they are not alone nor are they to blame for their experiences. **20 Years of Winter** is Marie's source of empowerment offered to those victims to stand up to their perpetrators and to speak out against victim shaming.

ABOUT THE PUBLISHER

Alas, who are we, marionettes on strings? And what do we stand for, puppeteers of our destiny?

I Ain't Your Marionette distinguishes itself as a stronghold of artistic liberation. At its helm, Marie Moldovan, once a marionette of circumstance, now orchestrates a symphony of narrative freedom. The company's sanctuary breathes life into marionette authors, whose tales of resilience and aspiration paint a vivid tableau of human spirit.

The press's hallmark anthologies, **Shattered Psyche** and **The Way of The Crow**, are more than mere collections; they are immersive experiences that beckon readers to venture beyond the mundane. Each story or visual masterpiece is a declaration of independence, a narrative that defies the norm and invites a reimagining of the world.

The **Voces Animarum** exhibition, alongside the **Shattered Psyche Traveling Showcase** and **Colours of Collaboration**, exemplifies the press's dedication to breaking new ground in literary and artistic expression. These ventures not only elevate the company's stature but also reverberate through the artistic community, transforming subdued creative murmurs into a powerful chorus that resonates far and wide.

FURTHER READING

***

Dive deeper into the captivating worlds crafted by Rick Powell. Each story in this collection explores the boundaries of love, loss, and the supernatural, inviting readers to confront their deepest fears and desires. Whether you're drawn to tales of obsession, apocalyptic nightmares, or chilling mysteries, there's something here for every lover of dark fiction.

Two Lost Souls:

Love, like life, is one of the oldest mysteries. But what happens when love turns into an obsession? When the boundaries between passion and madness blur, and the veil between the supernatural and natural world is cast aside? David believed his bond with his wife Helen was unbreakable, forged in the fires of life's trials. Yet, even the strongest love can be tested by the shadows that lurk in the corners of our hearts—and the darkness of a graveyard.

A Day of Ochre, Ascending:

In this apocalyptic nightmare inspired by Robert W. Chambers' The King in Yellow, a man's ordinary stroll with his dog turns into a nightmare. Each step plunges Walter and Archie deeper into a world of whispered doom. Will they escape, or will the nightmare consume them?

A Banquet of Panacea:

The loss of a child is a wound that never heals. But what if there was a way to move forward, a method so unthinkable it's only whispered about in the shadows? The Richards are living every parent's worst nightmare, their child's life stolen by a remorseless killer. In their darkest hour, they encounter Zhang, a billionaire with a chilling solution: when the justice system fails, he invites the families to a dinner shrouded in mystery and darkness.

Harold:

Frank is a seasoned detective with an uncanny 'feel' for things—a gift that has often guided him through the toughest cases. But this gift comes at a steep price. After years of risking his family and marriage for the job, Frank longs to slow down and reconnect with his loved ones.

However, fate has other plans. A mysterious journal lands in his hands, chronicling the twisted crimes of a madman named Harold. Is this a work of fiction, or a chilling true-life account of a delusional killer?

Winston:

Julie lives with her mother in a rundown part of town, struggling to adjust to her mom's new boyfriend, a man she distrusts for many reasons. During a fateful walk home, she encounters Winston, an enigmatic old man whose presence is as captivating as it is mysterious. As their bond deepens, Julie's life begins to change in unimaginable ways. Who is Winston, and what secrets does he hold that could lift Julie out of her adversity? Is he a savior, or a messenger of doom?

Ornament:

The holidays are a time for gathering with friends, family, and loved ones. Blazing fireplaces warm the bodies and hearts of those closest to us, as we share anecdotes of the year's events while the snow and bitter cold blow outside. But for Judith, the cold seeps inside her home, reflecting the turmoil in her life with John. Lies, cheating, and psychological abuse overshadow the season's joy, leaving her without a solution in sight.

Messages:

In a world where technology races forward, leaving yesterday's marvels in the dust, what if someone dared to blend ancient secrets with modern innovations? "Messages" delves into this terrifying possibility. Follow the harrowing journey of a reporter who uncovers the story of a lifetime—a story that could very well be his last.

As he digs deeper, he finds himself trapped in a web of dark forces and apocalyptic realities.

A Glimpse Beyond the Veil:

The final book, *A Glimpse Beyond the Veil*, brings together all seven stories. Within this anthology of shadows, secrets writhe through the corridors of forgotten places and sinister whispers shroud the night. Each tale lures readers into the abyss to confront their deepest fears. This collection is a haunting exploration of the human condition and beckons readers to step into a world where reality blurs with the supernatural.

Thank you for your support.